MONKEY KING

Journey to the West

Created by WEI DONG CHEN

Wei Dong Chen, a highly acclaimed and beloved artist, and an influential leader in the "New Chinese Cartoon" trend, is the founder of Creator World in Tianjin, the largest comics studio in China. Recently the Chinese government entrusted him with the role of general manager of the Beijing Book Fair, and his reputation as a pillar of Chinese comics has brought him many students. He has published more than three hundred cartoons, which have been recognized for their strong literary value not only in Korea, but in Europe and Japan, as well. Free spirited and energetic, Wei Dong Chen's positivist philosophy is reflected in the wisdom of his work. He is published serially in numerous publications while continuing to conceive projects that explore new dimensions of the form.

Illustrated by CHAO PENG

Chao Peng is considered one of Chen Wei Dong's greatest students, and is the director of cartoon at Creator World in Tianjin. One of the most highly regarded cartoonists in China today, Chao Peng's fantastic technique and expression of Chinese culture have won him the acclaim of cartoon lovers throughout China. His other works include "My Pet" and "Searching for the World of Self".

Original story

***"The Journey to The West"** by Wu, Cheng En*

Editing & Designing

Sun Media, Design Hongs, David Teez, Jonathan Evans, YK Kim, HJ Lee, SH Lee, Qing Shao, Xiao Nan Li, Ke Hu

Original Chinese edition published by Anhui Fine Arts Publishing House.

Characters

SAN ZANG

San Zang is a noble priest of the Tang Dynasty who, inspired by the Buddhist Goddess of Mercy and entrusted by Emperor TaiZong, undertakes a journey to the West in order to retrieve the sacred Buddhist Sutras that can save mankind. Raised in a Buddhist monastery from the time he was a baby, San Zang's past is filled with great sorrow and tragedy, yet he remains a very wise and compassionate person. His patience is tested, however, when he meets Sun Wu Kong, who is enlisted to become his apprentice on the journey. Now, San Zang must lead the way through a treacherous land of unknown adversity, while entrusting his safety to a disciple who has never had a fondness for taking orders.

JADE DRAGON

He is the third son of AoRun, the King of the West Sea. Like Sun Wu Kong, he caused a great deal of trouble in the heavens: in his case, he went on a rampage after learning of his wife's infidelity and set fire to a number of heavenly treasures. Branded a traitor, he was sentenced to death by the Jade Emperor, but his life was spared by the Goddess of Mercy, who enlists him to play an important role in Priest San Zang's journey. She transfigures him into a horse so that he can carry the priest to the West.

EMPEROR TAIZONG

Emperor TaiZong's real name was Li Shimin, and he was the second emperor of China's greatest era of prosperity, the Tang Dynasty. Born in 599, he ruled from 626 to 649. He was famous for, among other things, appointing officials based on talent, rather than privilege or social standing. In Journey to the West, Emperor TaiZong recruits Priest San Zang as an emissary of the Tang Dynasty, and dispatches him to the West in search of the Mahayana Sutras.

Characters

CHEN GUANG RUI

Chen Guang Rui is San Zang's father. He was a state official during the Tang Dynasty and assigned to govern Jiang District. On his way to take the assignment, he was thrown into the sea by a boatman named Liu Hong, who assumed his identity and stole his wife. However, he is rescued by the Sea King, who highly appraises his generous deed as an official.

PRIEST FA MING

After Liu Hong dispatched Chen Guang Rui, San Zang's mother put her newborn baby in a basket and sent it downriver to save his life. The basket eventually reached Mount Gold Temple, where Priest Fa Ming found the child and brought him to the temple to be raised. When San Zang was eighteen years old, Fa Ming revealed the truth of San Zang's origins, and the young priest left the temple to avenge his father and mother.

XIAO YU

According to The Journey to the West, he served as prime minister during the era of the Emperor TaiZong because he helped TaiZong a lot in his crowning. When the emperor held a Buddhist ceremony to widespread Buddhist teachings, he led the Buddhist Goddess of Mercy and her followers to the Emperor TaiZong. During the ceremony, Priest Xuan Zang volunteered to go to the West and was named San Zang.

AFTER BUDDHA BURIED SUN WU KONG UNDER FIVE-FINGER MOUNTAIN AND DECREED THAT HE REMAIN THERE FOR FIVE HUNDRED YEARS, THE JADE EMPEROR WAS DEEPLY GRATEFUL AND HELD A FEAST IN HIS HONOR.
THE GODDESS NIANG NIANG CAME ALONG WITH HER FAIRIES TO BESTOW FRESH PEACHES UPON THE BUDDHA AS A TOKEN OF APPRECIATION.

THE FEAST WAS A CELEBRATION OF THE PEACE IN HEAVEN, WHICH HAD BEEN MADE POSSIBLE BY THE DEFEAT OF THE IMPETUOUS MONKEY.

ALL THE SAINTS AND WIZARDS FROM THE SEAS, SKIES, AND CONTINENTS TO REJOICE...

Hmm...

BOOM
BOOM
BOOM
BOOM
That fat, disgusting cheater!
How can you call yourself a saint of great mercy and compassion after beating me with such a pathetic trick?

CREAK
Hrr...
Ack!
huff
huff
huff
SHOOOM
AFTER WATCHING SUN WU KONG LIFT UP FIVE-FINGER MOUNTAIN AND STICK HIS HEAD OUT, THE BUDDHA CALLED IN AH NUO AND GAVE HIM A CHARM.

AH
NUO
GROAN
You could put the weight of the world on my back, but you'll never be able to stop me!

What a stupid monster! So full of worldly desires and anger.
This charm contains the weight of universe. There is no way you can endure it.
HYAP
HRR HRR HRRM
Ha! I made it!
WHEESH

THUMP
SHUUNG
BOOM
BOOM
BOOM
Ugh!!!

AAHHH!!!!

BOOM

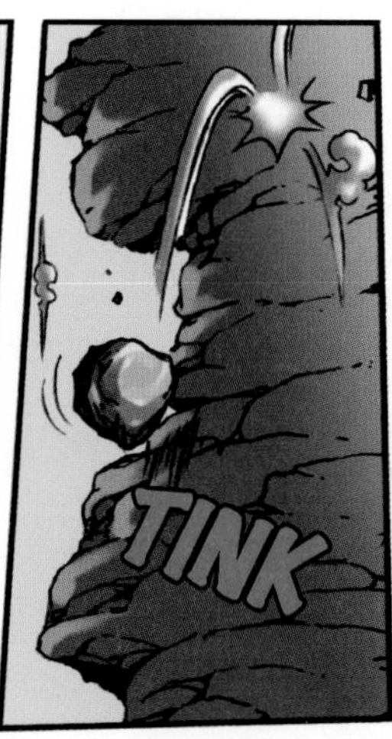
TINK

TONK

Now what?
Something's wrong!

I can't move an inch!

The Buddha must have played another trick on me.
Aw, come on!

You won't bring me to my knees in 500 million years, let alone 500 years!
The great Sun Wu Kong will not give up!

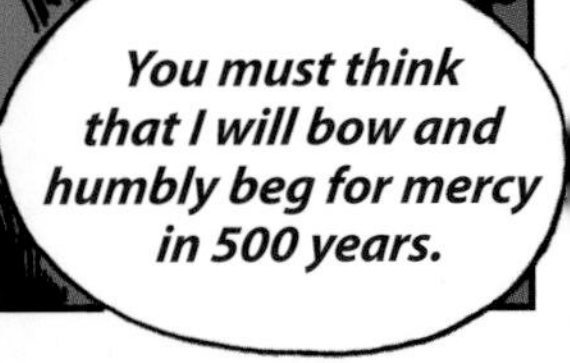
You must think 500 years is a long time.
You must think that I will bow and humbly beg for mercy in 500 years.

But my life span is as long as the life of Heaven. I'll simply take a nap for 500 years!

HA HA HA HA

ALTHOUGH, THIS MEANS I CAN'T SEE MY BROTHERS OR HAVE FUN WITH THEM FOR 500 YEARS...
...I CAN'T FLY AROUND THE WORLD ON CLOUDS...
I CAN'T TALK TO ANYONE UNLESS THEY COME TO ME...

UNTIL YESTERDAY, I RULED OVER
THE WHOLE WORLD AND MADE
ALL THE GODS OF HEAVEN AND EARTH
CRAWL ON MY FEET, BUT NOW...

No!!!
500 years is too long!
Buddha, you monster! Release me!
I won't do it again!
BUT IT WAS NO USE. BUDDHA'S JUDGMENT WAS FINAL, AND WU KONG WAS TO REMAIN THERE FOR 500 YEARS...
Let me out!
BUDDHA, MY BROTHER!
...BUT THE 500 YEARS COULD BE EXTENDED TO 5,000 YEARS OR 50,000 YEARS.

WITH SUN WU KONG OUT OF THE WAY, HEAVEN WAS FINALLY STABILIZED.
IN A WORLD WITHOUT THE HANDSOME MONKEY KING, TIME PASSED LIKE PEACEFUL RIVER WATER. BUT WHILE 500 YEARS MAY SEEM LIKE A BRIEF MOMENT IN TIME...
...IT SEEMED LONGER THAN AN ETERNITY TO THE MONKEY BURIED UNDER THE MOUNTAIN.

ONE DAY, AFTER COUNTLESS SEASONS HAD PASSED...

Twilight has fallen, the Milky Way dawns, the moon shines clear and bright...
CLOP
CLOP

...The sound of a wild goose echoes...

...The west wind is calling...

...A nesting bird yawns...
CLOP

...Chanting what the Buddha said until late at night...
...I have a long way to go.
Neigh!
neigh!

EMPEROR TAI ZONG OF THE TANG DYNASTY LEARNED THAT THE BUDDHIST GODDESS OF MERCY WAS LOOKING FOR SOMEONE TO RETRIEVE THE MAHAYANA BUDDHIST SUTRAS FROM INDIA TO FURTHER SPREAD THE WORD OF MAHAYANA BUDDHISM. THE PRIEST XUAN ZANG VOLUNTEERED TO GO, AND THE EMPEROR DECLARED HIM A BROTHER, RE-NAMING HIM SAN ZANG. SAN ZANG SET OUT FOR THE WESTERN HORIZON AND SOON ARRIVED AT A MOUNTAIN UNDER WHICH A MONKEY HAD BEEN PINNED HALF A MILLENNIUM.

What a strange looking mountain.

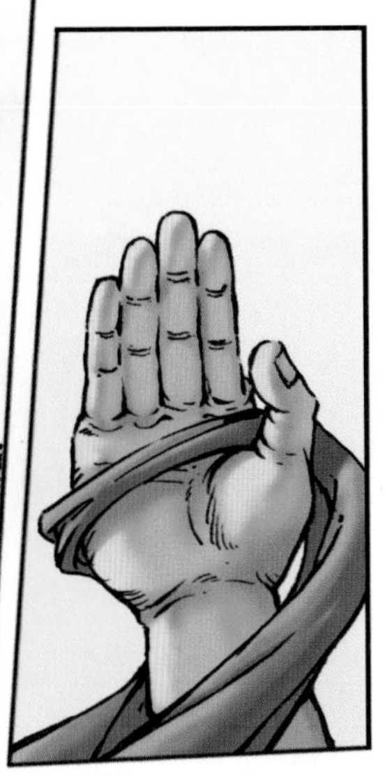

It looks like five extended fingers. A true rarity.
Hmm... Well, I guess...

...in a world this large, there are many odd places.

GRRRR
Easy, boy! Why have you stopped walking?

RAWR

Whoa!

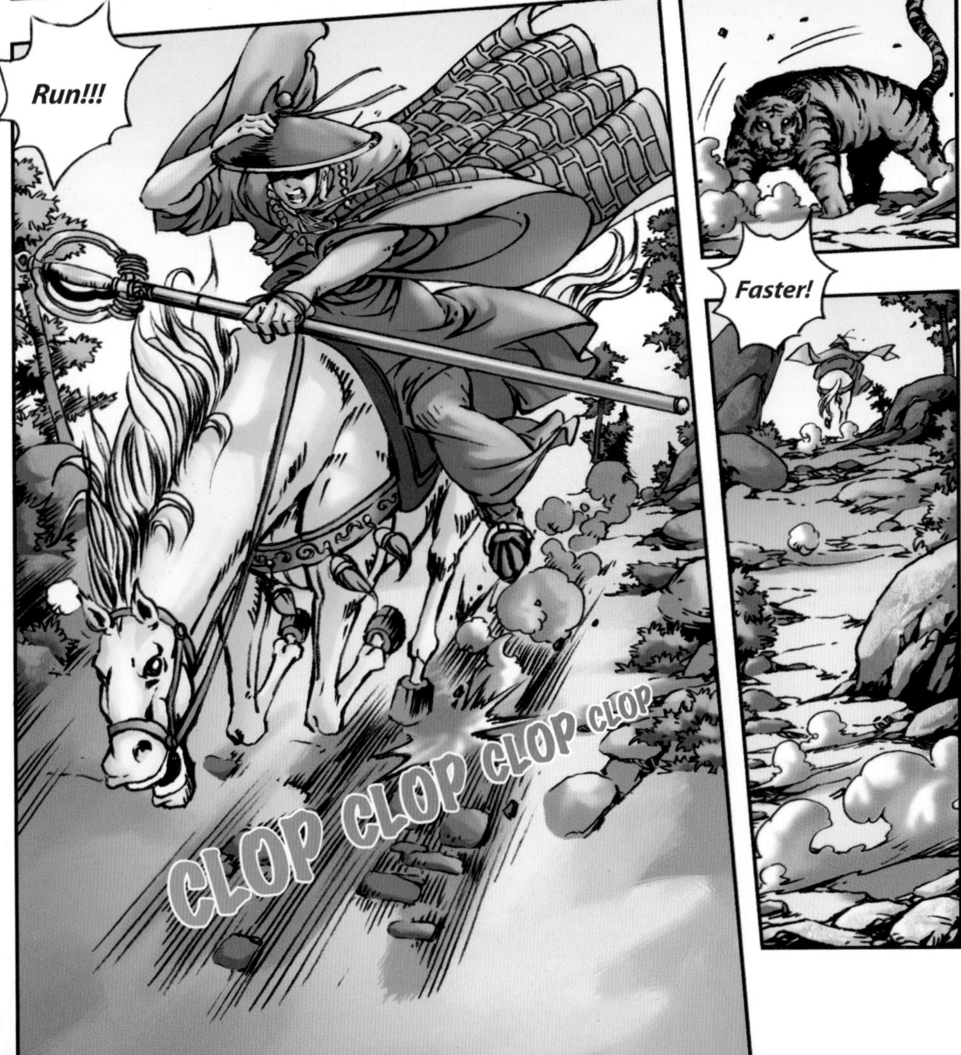
Run!!!
Faster!
CLOP CLOP CLOP CLOP

HUFF HUFF
huff, huff
Have we lost it?
That scared me
half to death!
!!!
Hoo hoo
hoo!
Eek!
Eek!

Hmm...

What a peculiar group of monkeys.
Why are they stopping me?

Easy, boy! What's happening?
Hoo hoo!
What are you saying?
Eek! Eek!

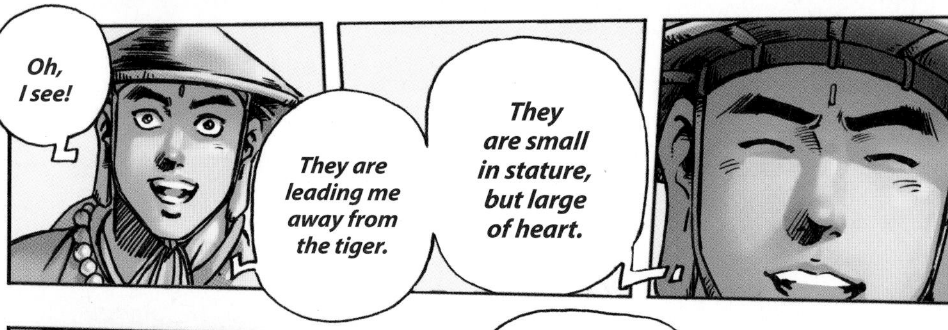
Oh, I see!
They are leading me away from the tiger.
They are small in stature, but large of heart.

Good monkeys! May you be born into health and strength in the next life.

Wait! Slow down!

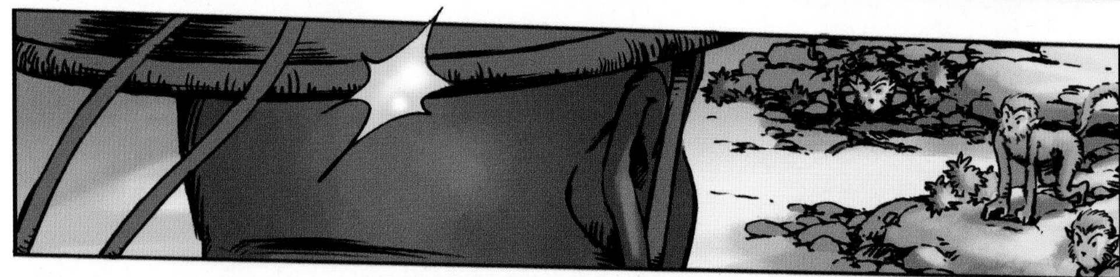

...

Remarkable. This monkey is pinned under the mountain…
...Yet he is still alive, and his eyes sparkle.

Master?
Master!

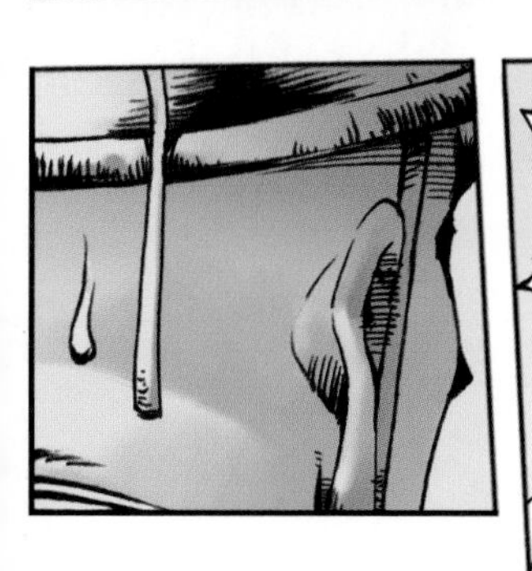

What the...
This monkey can speak!
UGH!
Don't be scared, Master!
Please listen to me! Here's what happened...

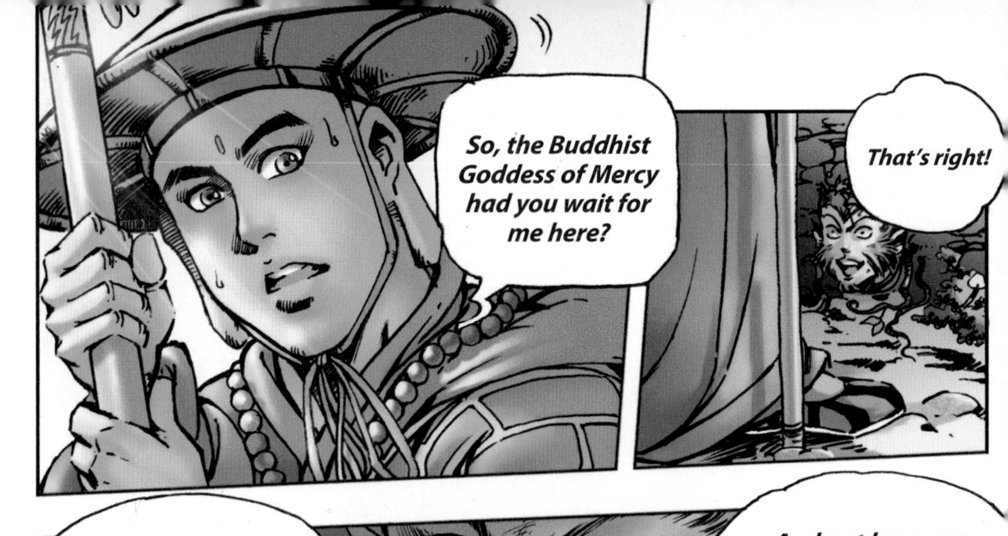
So, the Buddhist Goddess of Mercy had you wait for me here?
That's right!
I crossed the Buddha 500 years ago, and this was my punishment.
And not long ago, the Buddhist Goddess of Mercy told me I woul
have a chance to renoun
my evil deeds by doing a good deed.

She said that a master from the Tang Dynasty would pass by on his way to recover the Buddhist scriptures. She told me to accompany you to the West.
She said that?
So the Buddhist Goddess of Mercy performed an act of mercy... How fitting.
Yes, that's right. I have waited so long!

Master! Trust me! Let me guide you quickly and safely.
Please, let me out of here!

But I don't know how to get you out of here.
I can tell you.
At the top of the mountain is a charm made by the Buddha.
Just remove it, and I'll take care
of the rest.
But you have to get far away from the mountain after removing the charm. Otherwise, you might get hurt.

SWISH

Hya!
Let's get out of here!

That's right! Get as far away as possible.

At last, Sun Wu Kong is free!

CRUNCH

What? The mountain is shaking!
DM DM DM
DM
CREAK
ARRGH!!!

SHUAAAAHK

I don't believe it! I've never seen such a thing in my life!

How can this be?
Eek! Eek!

So, the Buddha's Five-Finger Mountain ...

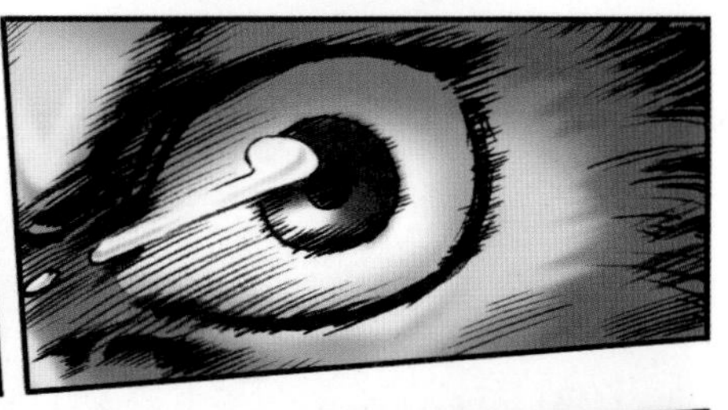

WHOOSH
I know right where you can shove this!

SWISH

!!!

At last...
SHUK
SHUK
SHUK
The Emperor of Heaven is back!!!

SHUWANG
HA HA HA
Clouds! Come here!
Ha ha ha!
How have you been these past 500 years?

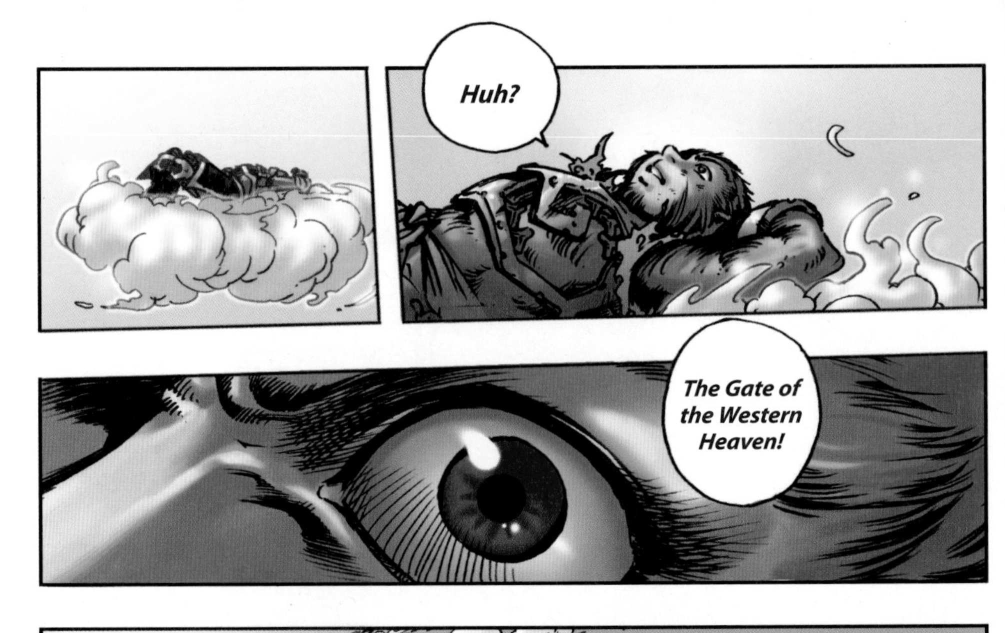
Huh?
The Gate of the Western Heaven!

I bet the Jade Emperor has had a good time since I've been gone.
Jerk.

I almost forgot! Master is waiting for me down there!

Master!
SWISH
Your disciple is here!
THUD

Master!
Please allow your disciple Sun Wu Kong's first bow.

Enough! Stand up. Your name is Sun Wu Kong?
Yes!
Master Puti gave me the Buddhist name Sun Wu Kong.

That's a very good name.
Since you look like...
...a young itinerant monk, let me give you another name.
What about Pilgrim Sun?
I like it!
The more names, the better.
By the way, your clothes look terrible.

Well, they once sparkled. But being buried under a mountain for 500 years will turn anything into rags.
So they don't look too good.
I have extra clothes you may wear.
That is very kind of you, Master.
Are you ready? Then mount your horse.

Let the journey begin!
THUMP THUMP
Ahh! Wu Kong! Wait a minute!

ZIP

Hey!

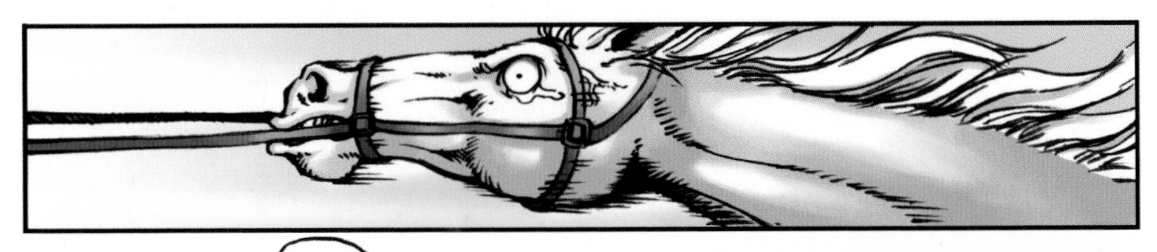

Please slow down!

Wu…Wu... Wu Kong…

WITH HIS NEW MASTER IN TOW, SUN WU KONG RAN LIKE THE WIND, AND THEY SOON ARRIVED AT THE RIM OF MOUNT GUI HANG.
Master! What a fantastic view!

Would you like to wait here for a while?

GASP
Wu Kong! Why did you run so fast?

You said that you were in a hurry.
Well, that was too fast.

I guess I've been pent up so long, I got carried away.
HA HA

Sun Wu Kong... You are quite talented and skillful.

You are strong enough to lift a mountain, as fast as lightening.
That seems to be why the Goddess of Mercy sent you to me.
Master, you shouldn't be so easily impressed.
I can travel thousands of miles by riding clouds. I have mastered 72 transfigurations. And I have defeated kings and monsters alike.
I'm very smart, and my military achievements are so great that I was once a god.
500 years ago...

...the army of the Jade Emperor could not beat me.
They came, I attacked, they ran away.
Why did the Jade Emperor send a heavenly army to kill you?
Because of that stupid old man!
The Jade Emperor cheated me out of what was mine!
So I decided to seize his throne!

What did you say?
You tried to overthrow the Jade Emperor?
Well, he angered me.
What?
Besides, he held out to the end...
By coaxing the Buddha into cheating me with a cheap trick.
The Buddha punished you in person?
You must have committed a grave sin.
Ha ha ha! You don't know the half of it!
If you're bored, I can tell you the story of my life.

Yes, yes?
Yes, yes.
I don't trust this creature.

First of all, I was born from a stone. So I don't have parents.

That's not all...

THMP

SPLASH

SLURP
SLURP

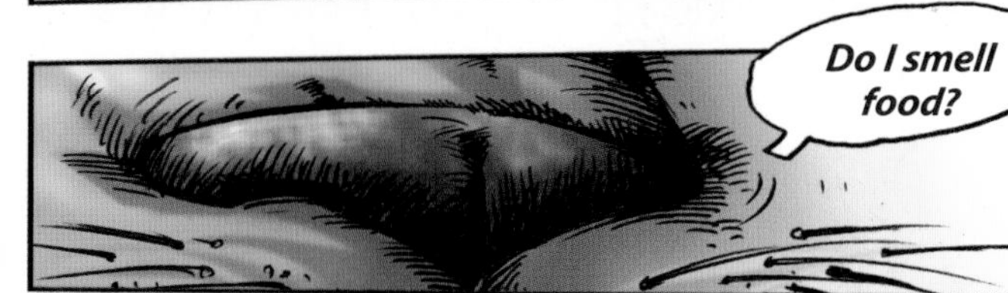
Do I smell food?

...

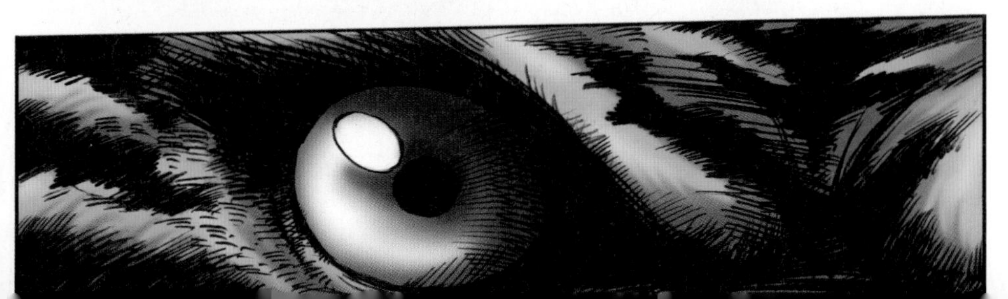

...and that's why I was pinned under that mountain for 500 years.
That's incre-dible!
To be honest with you, it sucked.
Does he really think I believe him?
On the other hand, he has kept intact after being pinned under a mountain, so I can't help but believe him.
And if he's telling the truth...
Heh, the stupid Buddha!
I'm in big trouble!

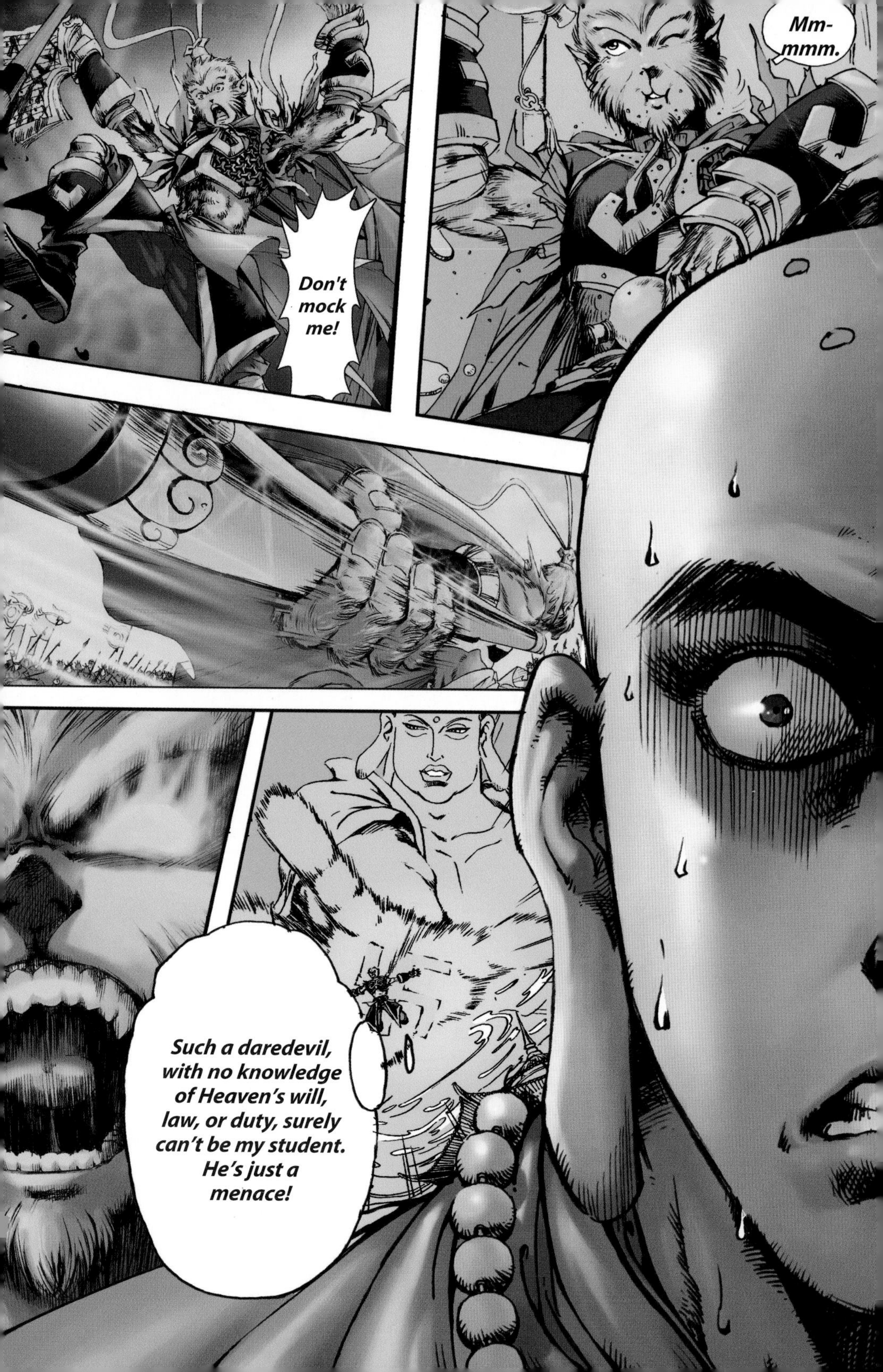
Mm-
mmm.
Don't
mock
me!
Such a daredevil, with no knowledge of Heaven's will, law, or duty, surely can't be my student. He's just a menace!

Even though he spent 500 years under a mountain and may regret his sins…

…his true character could be revealed at any time.

Master, what are you thinking so hard about?
Gahh!!!
Oh, no! My rice bowl!

SWOOSH

PLUCK

Here you go.
This is your means of living.
You should be more careful.
Oh, yes. Thanks.
I just got so carried away by your story...

GRRRR
GRRR

Master is really terrified. Ha ha ha!

Gahh!!!
Tiger!

RAWR
What's the matter?
Are you afraid of a cat?

GRRAAHHH

Here, kitty. My new clothes have arrived just in time.

Yah!

WHAP

CRUNCH

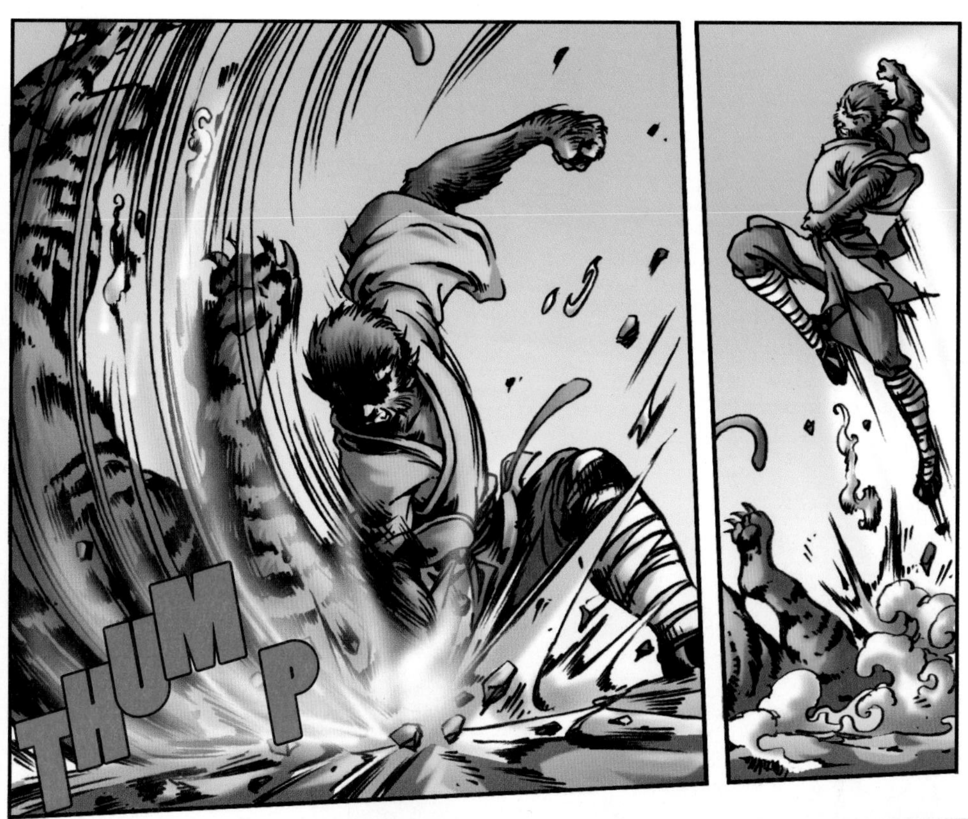
THUMP

Thanks for the wardrobe!
WHAM

Save us,
merciful
Buddha.
Why did you kill
the tiger instead of
just making it
go away?

Making it go away?
This walking clothes rack came right at me.
It's not a clothes rack. It was a tiger.
No, it's an outfit.
See? Don't I look handsome?

Hmm...
It looks
good enough,
I suppose.
If you find
a place to rest,
I will sew them up
for you.

Master?
I am a genius,
but there is
something
I don't
understand.
Why are you
going through
so much trouble
to fetch some trifling
Buddhist scriptures
from India?

Sun Wu Kong …
Really?
I am just doing as the Goddess of Mercy commanded.
I have no clue.
Do you know what kind of Buddhist scriptures we are trying to get, and what they can teach us?
I don't understand why everybody makes such a fuss about some trivial scriptures.

What the heck are those?

They are the Mahayana Sutras.

"THE NAME OF EMPEROR TAI ZONG OF TANG DYNASTY IS LI SHI MIN."
"HE LED A LARGE MILITARY FORCE TO CONQUER HIS ENEMIES AT A YOUNG AGE, AND ALL THE PEOPLE PRAISED HIS NAME."

"HOWEVER, HE FELL ILL SOON AFTER HE TOOK THE THRONE AND PASSED AWAY. IN DEATH, HE WAS ABLE TO SEE ALL THE EVIL IN THE UNIVERSE."

"BUT ONE OF HIS SUBJECTS, NAMED WEI ZHENG, CONSPIRED WITH HIS FRIEND CUI JUE TO REVIVE THE EMPEROR FROM THE UNDERWORLD."

"WHEN HE RETURNED, THE KING BECAME OBSESSED WITH HUMAN VIRTUE. YEARS LATER, HAVING BEEN CONVERTED TO BUDDHISM AS A CHILD, I WAS PRESENTED TO THE EMPEROR."

"RIGHT AWAY, THE EMPEROR COULD SEE THAT I SHARED HIS NEED TO SPREAD GOODNESS AND VIRTUE, AND I BECAME HIS TRUSTED EMISSARY."
"AFTER RECEIVING THE DOCTRINE OF THE EMPEROR, I WENT TO HUA SHENG TEMPLE TO SPREAD THE TEACHINGS OF BUDDHA."
"ONE DAY, THE EMPEROR'S PRIME MINISTER, XIAO YU, NOTICED TWO PRIESTS WITH LEPROSY WHO WERE SELLING MONKS' ROBES AND STAFFS. HE THOUGHT I MIGHT NEED THEM."
Hmm...
Do you want to buy these?
The robe costs 5,000 and the staff costs 2,000.
"XIAO YU BROUGHT THE MONKS BEFORE EMPEROR TAI ZONG, AND WHEN I MENTIONED NEEDING WHAT THEY WERE SELLING, THE MONKS OFFERED THEM TO ME FOR FREE. WE WERE PERPLXED, BUT THE MONKS LEFT THE GIFTS AND VANISHED."

"EMPEROR TAI ZONG PRESENTED THE TWO PIECES OF TREASURE TO ME, AND THEN VISITED MY TEMPLE AND BURNED INCENSE EVERY DAY DURING A 49-DAY BUDDHIST CEREMONY. ONE DAY, WHILE GIVING A SERMON, I SAW THE TWO MONKS WITH LEPROSY IN THE CROWD."
Thank you for your Hinayana teachings.
But do you know the Mahayana teachings?
Did you say the Mahayana teachings?

"IT WAS THEN THAT THE MONKS SHOWED THEIR TRUE SELVES, AND THE EMPEROR RECOGNIZED THEM: THEY WERE THE BUDDHIST GODDESS OF MERCY AND THE PILGRIM, HUI AN."
"THEY WISHED TO RETRIEVE THE MAHAYANA SUTRAS, WHICH COULD END HUMANITY'S EVIL AND BRING VIRTUE TO THE WORLD."
"I IMMEDIATELY VOLUNTEERED FOR THE MISSION. GREATLY PLEASED, THE EMPEROR EMBRACED ME AS A BROTHER."

You said that the countries bordering western China are only a few thousands miles from here? I can get you those sutras right now!

It would only take a moment!

Wu Kong!

The deep spiritual enlightenment of Buddha cannot be--
--reached without dedication, and one does not achieve this by taking the easy path.

Well, it sounds like a waste of time.
"Save us, merciful Buddha." Pish!

By the way, you said that you became a Buddhist monk as a child.
Did your parents abandon you at a temple when you were born?
It sounds cruel.
HA HA HA
Compared to you, I was born under a lucky star!
...
Master ...?

Shut up and keep moving.

I guess he doesn't want to talk about it.

SAN ZANG AND WU KONG WOKE EARLY IN THE MORNING AND JOURNEYED WELL INTO THE NIGHT TO REACH INDIA AS SOON AS POSSIBLE. ONE DAY...

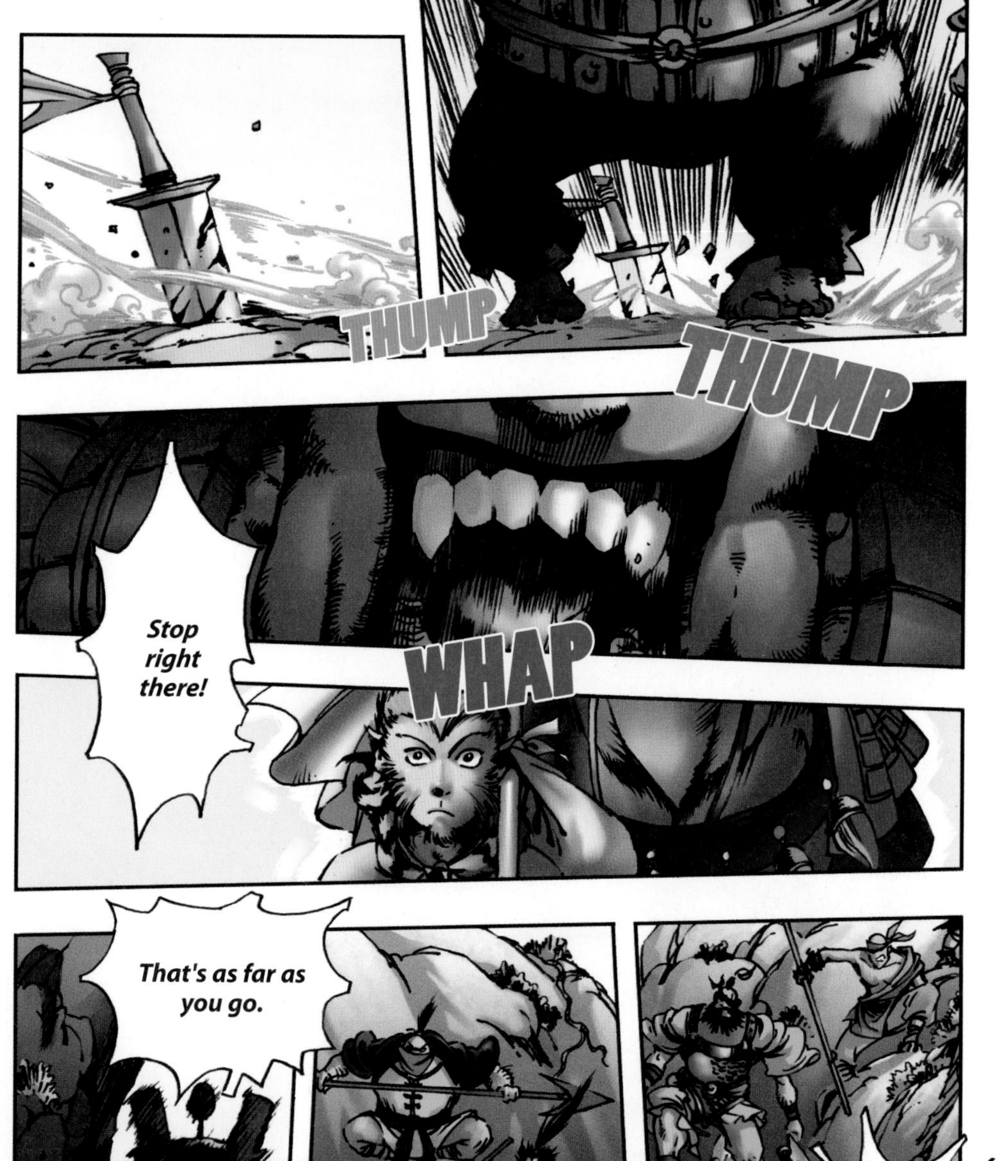
THUMP
THUMP
Stop right there!
WHAP

That's as far as you go.
HA HA HA
If you value your life--
--hand over your possessions and run away.

Don't just stand there!
Do you really want us
to take them by force?
HA HA HA

Ahh!
WHUMP

Wu Kong, What should we do?

Mind your tongue, you little turd. I am the supreme king of this mountain.

Don't worry! I can easily crush a few pests.

I am known on several mountains, but I've never even heard of you.
What did this small thing say?

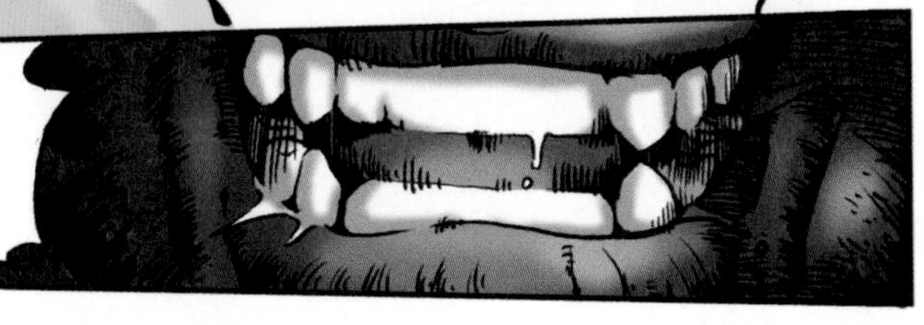
Our very names will strike terror in your heart.

I am Yan Kan Xi!

I'm She Chang Si!
I'm Bi Chui Ai!

I'm Er Ting Nu!
I'm Yi Jian Yu!

And I am Shen Ben You!

Uh, boss, is he laughing at us?
Why you little--

You little turd! What are you laughing at?
CLANG
Uh, boss? Did you get a cheapie?

Crush him!
CLANK
You can't avoid my blow this time!!!

CRUNCH
Ahem...
Are we done?

Then I guess it's my turn.
What on earth is this little rodent?

PLUCK

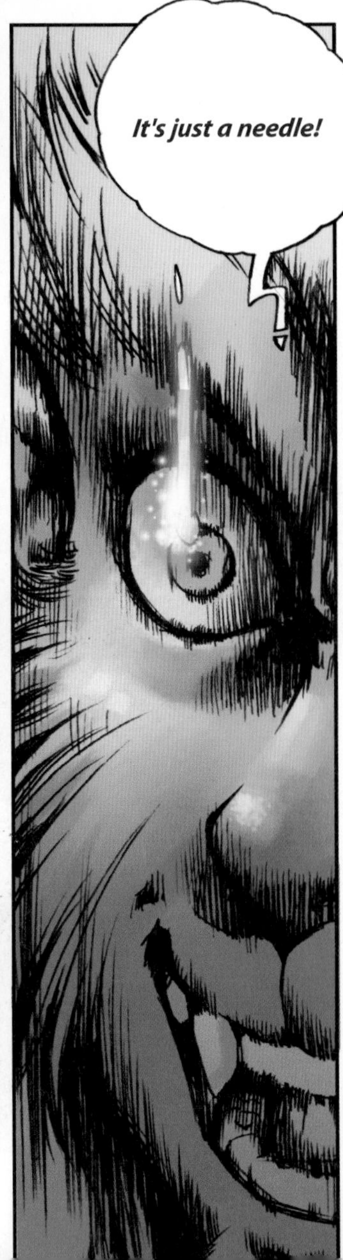
It's just a needle!

HA HA
I haven't used this in 500 years.

It's just a needle.
HA HA HA HA

WHOOOSH
...Powerful enough to harden the earth of the sea!
WHAM

HA HA HA HA
Trusty as ever.
In fact, I should use this sparingly.
Wu Kong, where did the bandits go?
Where do you think they went?
HA HA HA HA
I pulverized them with a single blow!
With a single blow?
His vicious nature is still intact!

You stupid monkey! Even the lives of bandits are precious!
Nah, they would have harassed others.
Then you should have turned them over to the authorities. There is never a good--
--reason to take a life. A Buddhist must have a merciful heart.
Why do you insist on killing?
...
Because your heart is full of ugliness!

Mine is one life, but you have now killed six people.
It goes beyond all reason. What will happen if the authorities find out?

You were so brutal that the Buddha--
--punished you for 500 years.
If you can't escape such violent impulses, you shouldn't go to India!
That sounds good! It seems better to me not to go there at all!!

sigh
This is hope-less.
Fine! Do it yourself!
SWOOSH

What a petulant--
Why is it so hard for him to learn?
And how can he be so angry after such a minor scolding?
So it be.
I am not supposed to have a disciple anyway.
I should go by myself.
Save us, merciful Buddha.
This is my fault... All my fault.

SAN ZANG PACKED UP HIS THINGS AND LOADED THEM ON HIS HORSE BEFORE HEADING WEST ALONE. SAN ZANG CUT A SOLITARY FIGURE, AND BEFORE LONG…
Excuse me. Who are you?
I'm under orders from the emperor of Tang Dynasty, and am on my way to the west to find Mahayana Sutras.

Why are you journeying so far without anyone accompanying you?
As a matter of fact, I had a disciple--
--but he had a fiery temper.
He fled after I disciplined him.
That explains why you're alone.
Not the best disciple, eh?

Don't worry. He will be back soon enough.

If he does come back though--

--how will I deal with him? He may show his true colors again.

Should that happen,
I have a gift for you.
If you make the most of it,
your student will
obey you.

Really?

MEANWHILE,
SUN WU KONG HAD
FLED FOR THE EAST
SEA, AND EVENTUALLY
REACHED THE PALACE
OF THE SEA KING.

Oh, hello, Sun Wu Kong. Help yourself.
Ha ha This is very good!
MUNCH
MUNCH
I haven't stuffed myself in centuries...
Yes, I heard that you were buried under a mountain.
First--
--let me congratulate you on your escape.
So... Rumor has it that you're accompanying San Zang to the West.
Why are you here without him?

Dang! Now I've lost my appetite!
What happened?
Don't mention that coward!
We met some bandits on a mountain, so I crushed them to death with the miracle staff!
Then he chewed me out for being so violent!
So I ditched him.
I'm only saying this for caution's sake...
...But, it seems you've made a big mistake.

Why do you say that?

If you have decided to become a Buddhist,
you are obligated to have mercy.
If you do whatever you want, as you did in the past, the Buddha might...
...
This may be your palace, but I'm not in the mood to listen to--
--your criticism after just listening to that blowhard of a monk.
It was bad enough having to deal with him! Now you, too?
You'd better be careful from now on!

Now, wait a second!!
Emperor of Heaven!
I didn't mean to offend you.

Please don't be so angry. I won't mention it ever again.
You promise?
Sure.
Ha! It's like we're brothers!
Friends for more than 500 years, yes?

Wow!
What a a fantastic pearl!
Sea King!
May I? I'd like to hang it up at Spring Mountain.
Umm, I'm sorry but...
Wow! This drawing is gorgeous! What is it?
Oh! It took place after you were imprisoned.
It's the story of what happened to Zhang Liang.
It 's titled "PiQiao SanJinLu."
The Taoist hermit in the drawing is Huang Shi Gong, and the young man is Zhang Liang--
--who eventually became Prime Minister. One day, Huang Shi Gong was walking on a bridge and dropped his shoe down under the bridge three times.

Each time, he asked Zhang Liang to pick it up and put it back on him. Each time, Zhang Liang put the shoe back on without any complaints.

Greatly impressed with Zhang Liang's character, Huang Shi Gong took him as a student.

Zhang Liang learned much and made great contributions when Liu Bang founded a dynasty.
!!!
Unless you serve San Zang diligently--
--you will never find enlightenment, and you will end up a monster.

He's right!
The Goddess of Mercy
also said that I wouldn't
find enlightenment
unless I converted to Buddhism
with sincerity and conviction!
Umm...
Umm...
Thanks,
Sea King!
See you later!
Yes, well,
if you're
busy...
Time
flies!
I must
return to
Spring
Mountain.
If you
say
so...

sigh
Thank heaven he's gone.

I barely managed to keep the precious pearl.
SWOOSH

Thank God! If I hadn't seen that drawing--
--I would have missed out on enlightenment and miraculous powers.

!
Oh, great. The Buddhist Goddess of Mercy.
WU KONG! I TOLD YOU TO ACCOMPANY SAN ZANG.
WHAT ARE YOU DOING HERE?
I, em, well...
I went to get some food.
I'm about to return.
IS THAT SO? I WILL BELIEVE YOU THIS TIME...

BUT GO BACK RIGHT AWAY BEFORE SOMETHING HAPPENS TO HIM.
Yes, Goddess! Right away.

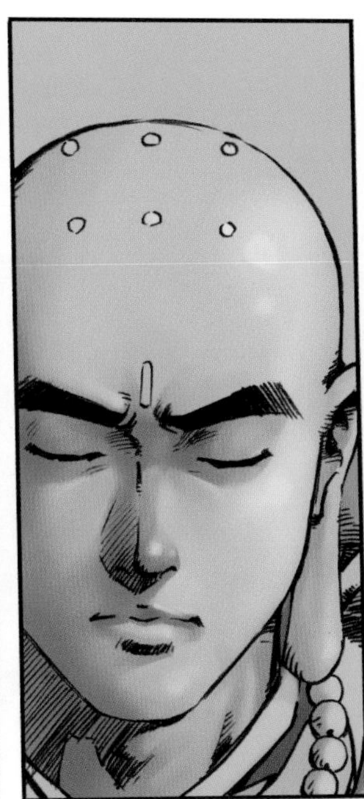

Master!

Master! What are you doing here?

Didn't you say you were busy?
I'm waiting for you.
Where have you been and
where would I have gone without you?
Eh--

I went to the Sea King to get some food for you.
The Sea King?
A Buddhist monk is not supposed to lie under any circumstances.
How did you visit the East Sea in such a short time?
I tried to tell you.

I can fly thousands of miles in a moment!
If you have such miraculous power,
why did you leave me alone in the vast wilderness?

I told you. I went for food.
I don't need food!
I have food in my bundle. Bring it to me.

Yes, Master!
Huh?

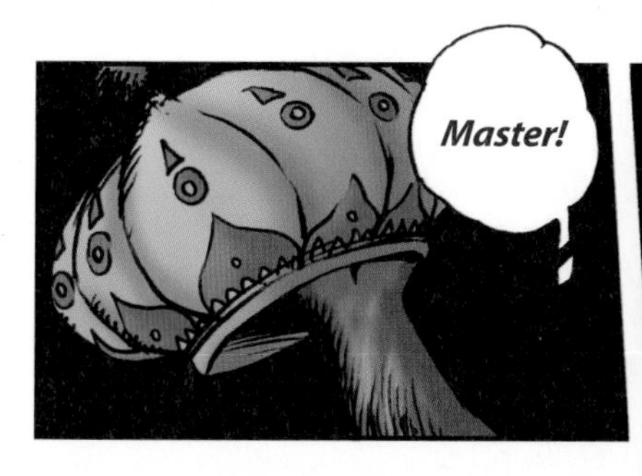
Master!

Do you wear this hat?

I wore it when I was a child.
If you put it on, you can find enlightenment without learning the Buddhist scriptures. Do you want to try?

Yes!

I really like it!
Wow!

HA HA HA
WAHOO
Ahh!!!

Ugh!
My head hurts!
It's giving me a
splitting headache!
Ohh...
A
headband?
Why am I
wearing a
headband?
You cannot
be serious.

Argh!
It won't come off!
Get it off me!
Hrr!
If he takes it off, I'm in big trouble.
Band of gold...
Do not let go ...
His will to harm will not hold...
If pain can make it so...
Stop him now!

Ugh!

Ack!!!

!
What... What was that?
Were you casting a spell?
Hrr...
I was uttering a JinGuZhou incantation.
If you make any trouble again, I say the incantation. Do you understand?

Okay, Master!
I will obey you.

Do you promise to behave from now on?

I promise.

SHIK—

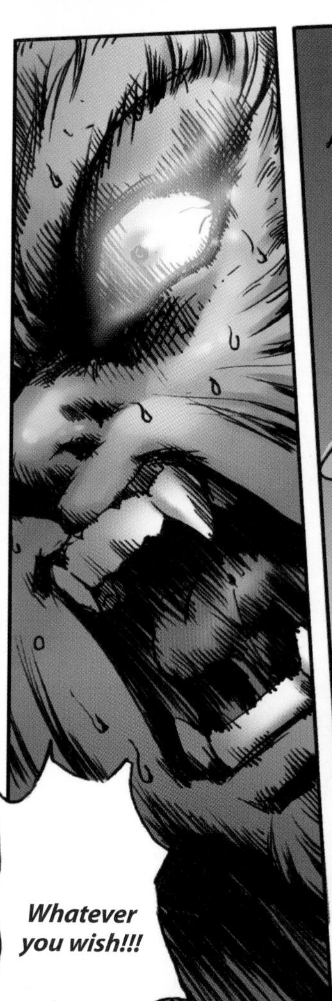
Whatever you wish!!!

Now you're a dead man!

SWOAK

Band of gold, do not let go!
His will to harm will not hold...
If pain can make it so...
Oww! My head! My head!
Ouch... I'm sorry!
What a bad monkey!
How dare you try to hit me!
No, I'm just...
I was just going to ask where you got this headband.
An old lady gave it to me. Why? Are you planning to chase after her for revenge?

An old lady?

No wonder the Goddess of Mercy was hanging around!

I will go to the South Sea to give her a piece of my mind!
What a fool! Don't you understand that she was the one

who taught me the incantation? If she utters the spell, you are as good as dead.

Where are you going?
Where do you think I'm going?

I don't believe this!
There is no way out of this!
Okay. I will obey you from now on. Please don't cast the spell.
If you act respectfully, I won't have to.
I despise you, and the Goddess of Mercy.

AFTER GATHERING THEIR CAMP, SUN WU KONG AND SAN ZANG CONTINUED ON THEIR JOURNEY TO FIND THE BUDDHIST SCRIPTURES.

WHOOSH
SPLISH

SPLISH
THEY HAD A LONG WAY TO GO BEFORE REACHING THE WEST...

...AND SAN ZANG LOOKED DEPRESSED THE ENTIRE TIME.

AS NIGHT FELL, THEY FOUND A PLACE TO SLEEP. EVEN WHEN EVERYONE ELSE WAS ASLEEP, SAN ZANG KEPT TOSSING AND TURNING IN BED AND COULDN'T GO TO SLEEP.

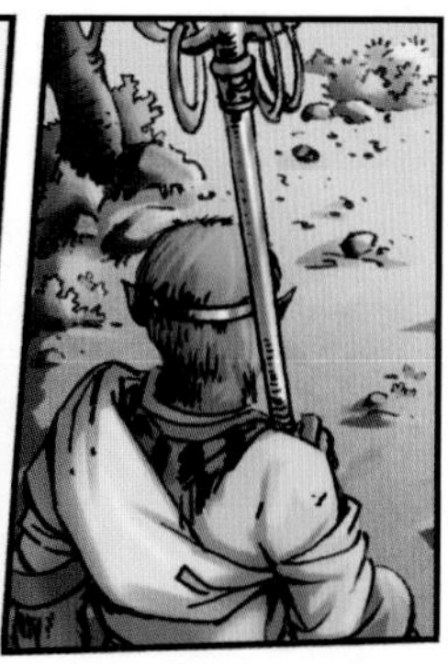

Wu Kong!

Yes, Master?
You asked about my past.
Do you want to hear about it?

Yes, I do. What would you like to tell me?

Hmm …
Let me tell you about my father.

MY FATHER'S FAMILY NAME WAS CHEN, AND HIS FIRST NAME WAS GUANG RUI.
狀元及第
HE WAS SO TALENTED THAT HE WON FIRST PLACE IN A STATE EXAMINATION BEFORE BEING APPOINTED AS AN OFFICIAL TO GOVERN JIANG DISTRICT.
ONE DAY, WHILE HE WAS CROSSING A RIVER, A BOATMAN CALLED LIU HONG, WHO HAD FALLEN IN LOVE WITH MY MOTHER, PUSHED HIM OVERBOARD.
Ha ha ha! Go to hell! I will take your wife and your government post.

LIU HONG STOLE MY FATHER'S IDENTITY AND WENT TO JIANG DISTRICT. MY MOTHER WAS PREGNANT WITH ME AT THE TIME AND HAD NO CHOICE BUT TO FOLLOW HIM.

BEFORE LONG, MY MOTHER GAVE BIRTH TO ME, PUT ME IN A BASKET AND SET IT AFLOAT IN THE RIVER BEFORE HE HURT ME.
WAA
WAA

WAA
WAA

WAA
WAA
WAA

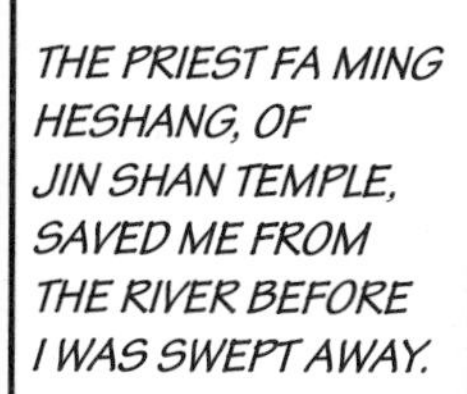
THE PRIEST FA MING HESHANG, OF JIN SHAN TEMPLE, SAVED ME FROM THE RIVER BEFORE I WAS SWEPT AWAY.

THE PRIEST FA MING HESHANG
Oh, my.

PRIEST FA MING FOUND THE NOTE MY MOTHER HAD WRITTEN IN HER OWN BLOOD AND PINNED TO MY CHEST, WHICH EXPLAINED WHAT HAD HAPPENED.

WHEN I HAD GROWN UP, PRIEST FA MING SHOWED ME THE BASKET AND MY MOTHER'S NOTE, WHICH REVEALED THE SECRET OF MY BIRTH.

AFTER CRYING BITTERLY, I CLIMBED DOWN THE MOUNTAIN TO SEEK REVENGE FOR MY FATHER AND SAVE MY MOTHER.

Huh?

Why did she do that when the family had been restored?

WHILE THE TWO WERE TALKING
ABOUT SAN ZANG'S PAST,
THEY REACHED YING CHOU GULLY
AT MOUNT SHE PAN.

This road is pretty rocky. You'd better get off the horse.

PLOP
PLOP
SWISH
SWOOSH
!

Wow, a dragon!
neigh

Only three?
Not even an appetizer.
CLANG
Well, better than nothing.
Master! Watch out!
My feet...
Can't move... So scared!
CRUNCH
Wu Kong! Help me!!!

Wait a minute...
Where did
they go?

Master!
Don't just
hang there
like a corpse!
I can't
fly like
this!

gasp, gasp
Wu Kong! Was that thing real?
I was so terrified when I saw... that ...that dragon.
I almost took a tour of his stomach!
Can't seem to steady myself...
Crazy beast. How dare it consider me as a meal?
Where's our horse?
Dragon food.
There was only time to save one of you...
I can go back to cut the dragon open and retrieve the horse.

SNAG
Wu Kong! If you're gone…
What?
What if the dragon comes to get me?
Why don't you make up my mind already?
Do you want me to get the horse or not?
Jeez!
EMPEROR OF HEAVEN! PLEASE GO EASY!
Who are you?
SHOOOM
!

WE WILL PROTECT SAN ZANG--
--WHILE YOU GO GET THE HORSE.

All right. Take good care of the master.

SWOOSH

Who are these people?
If anything happens to the master, you will answer to me!!

IN TRUTH, THE DRAGON WAS THE SON OF THE SEA KING, AO RUN. HE HAD BEEN SENTENCED TO DEATH BY THE KINGDOM OF HEAVEN, BUT WAS EXILED TO THE SEA THANKS TO THE WISDOM OF THE GODDESS OF MERCY.

WHOOSH

Where is that wretched horse?

The stupid dragon must have digested it already!

Hey, tadpole!
Show yourself!

WHOOSH
Hi there, minnow. Give me back my horse!

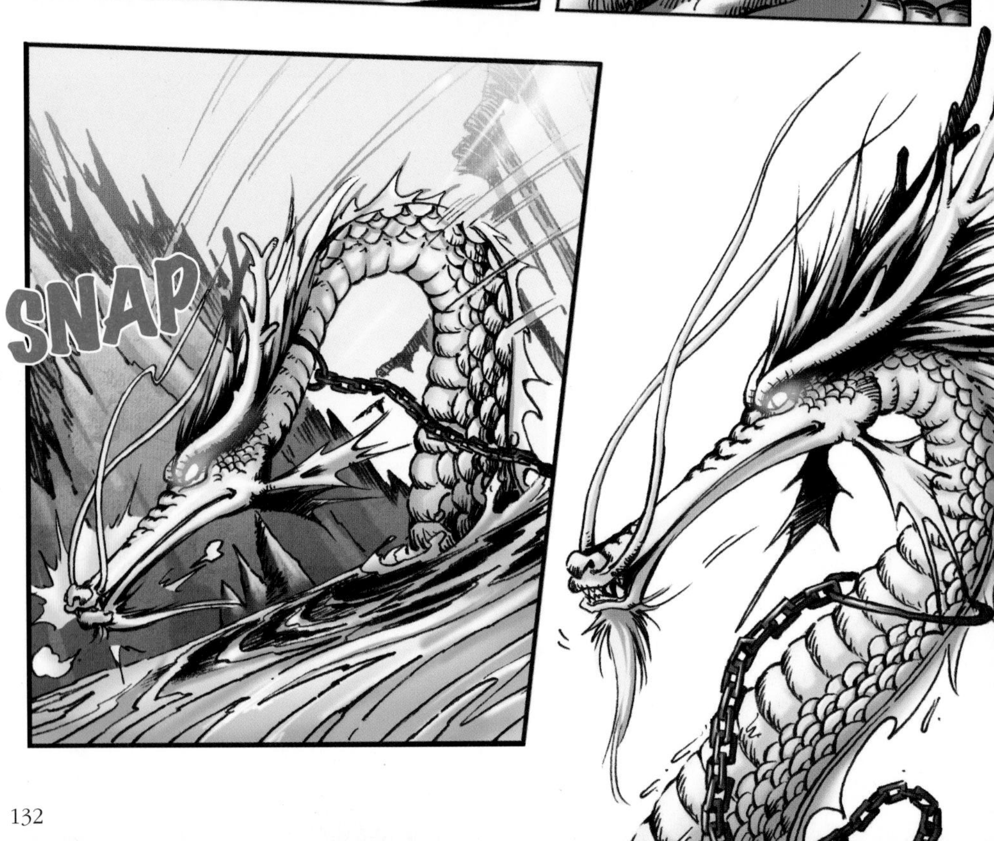
SNAP

!!!
CRACK
Hey, shark bait. Have you ever heard of toothbrush? It reeks in here.
Fine. I will let the miracle staff clean you out.

GROW!

How's that taste? Refreshing?
SHOOM
SWISH–

Ha ha ha! Had enough?
Want some more?
Look, a dragon kebab!

SHINK

Wait a minute. How did it escape? This is no ordinary dragon.
How can I find it?
The horse has
disappeared, and the dragon
has run away like a coward after being beaten by me.
You mean the dragon has the horse?
Hmm…
Didn't you say that you can beat monsters? How can you fail to recover a horse?
Wu Kong?
Have you found the horse?

And how am I supposed to get to the West? On foot?
Oh, don't be such a wimp.
Fine. I will go back and get the horse this time.
SWOOSH
Hey, minnow! The bell tolls for you!

Come on, you slimy fish!
Show yourself! My master scolded me because of you!
SPLISH
I will turn this pond upside down!

SHOOWA

Huh?
Now it's
a person?
You little
piece of
scum!
Who
do you think
you are?
Shut up and
give me back
my horse!
Here, take
what's left!

Filthy reptile!
HWACK
Today will be your last on Earth!

CLANG

THUNG
CWANK

SHWAK

He's too much!
I must flee
for now.

SWISH
WHOOSH

That's the fastest retreat
I've ever seen.

How am I supposed to find him?
You cowardly reptile! Show yourself!
What a fool...
I don't have a death wish.

Where is Sun Wu Kong?

I've never seen such a huge creature so easily scared off.

Goddess of Mercy?
Emperor of Heaven!
We asked her to help us.

Good. I have a bone to pick with her anyway.

Why did you bother putting this thing on my head?
I already told you that I would help San Zang get the Buddhist scriptures.

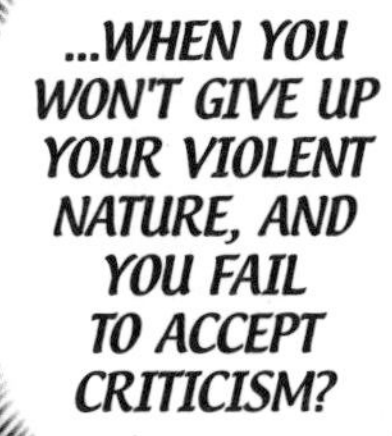
Every time he casts a spell, I get a splitting headache!
HOW CAN I TEACH YOU...
...WHEN YOU WON'T GIVE UP YOUR VIOLENT NATURE, AND YOU FAIL TO ACCEPT CRITICISM?

What a crock!
IF YOU DO THE RIGHT THING, THE HEADBAND WON'T HURT YOU AT ALL...

Fine. Now, tell me, why is there a dragon living here?
I ASKED THE JADE EMPEROR TO SEND THE DRAGON FOR SAN ZANG.

What? You sent the dragon?

AN ORDINARY HORSE WON'T BE ABLE TO SURVIVE THE JOURNEY TO THE WEST.

YOU NEED AN EXTRAORDINARY CREATURE, LIKE THE DRAGON.

THE DRAGON WAS THE SON OF THE KING OF THE WEST SEA. HE DISCOVERED THAT HIS WIFE WAS HAVING AN AFFAIR WITH A MONSTER--
--WITH NINE HEADS. SO HE FOUGHT THE MONSTER, AND BURNED EVERY TREASURE IN THE SEA KING'S PALACE. HE WAS BRANDED AS A TRAITOR.

The poor thing. He's been abandoned by his wife and his father...
WU KONG!
What?
THESE THREE HAIRS CAN SAVE LIFE.

I GIVE THEM TO YOU FOR USE IN AN EMERGENCY.
Downy hairs that can save life?
Ha ha ha! Alright, I will forgive you for the headband. Let's call it even.
Hmm.

THE GODDESS OF MERCY SUMMONED THE JADE DRAGON AND TURNED IT INTO A DRAGON HORSE.
SUN WU KONG RETURNED TO SAN ZANG WITH THE DRAGON HORSE, AND THEY CONTINUED THEIR JOURNEY TO THE WEST.
Oh! This is extraordinary !

Wow!
He doesn't run out of breath, and he's as fast as the wind.
So fast!!
SAN ZANG, NOW RIDING THE DRAGON HORSE, COULD KEEP UP WITH WU KONG. EVENTUALLY, THEY ARRIVED AT A BUDDHIST TEMPLE.
CLANG, CLANG, CLANG

At last! A Buddhist temple.
It must be the Goddess of Mercy's temple.
Wu Kong! Bring my hat.
Yes, master!
We give thanks to the Goddess of Mercy for her gifts on this journey.
Master! Why don't you wear the monk's robe?

It is too precious to wear casually. I must keep it safe.
I don't understand.

I'm to wear it only when in the company of a king or the Buddha in the West.

Yeesh. What a waste! You would look graceful in it!

觀音殿
CLANG~

CLANG~
CLANG~
CLANG~
CLANG~
CLANG~
CLANG~
CLANG~
CLANG~
CLANG~
CLANG~
CLANG~
What the? Who is that?
This is not the time to ring the bell!

CLANG~
CLANG~
Woohoo!
What a wicked monkey!
Come down here right now!
!
Who do you think you are?
Who do you think I am? I am the Emperor of Heaven.

Ugh! It's a monkey!
It's a talking monkey!
It must be a monster!
Who just called me a monster?
I am Sun Wu Kong, and I don't like insults.
What a nuisance.
Wu Kong! Behave yourself!
Chief Priest! I come from the Tang Dynasty in the East.
We are going to the West. May we stay the night?
Who is this monkey… no, sorry, this person?
He is Pilgrim Sun!
Hello.

Please come inside and have some tea.
Thank you for your hospitality.
My word! Such a beautiful cup!
You're very generous with your compliments.
As I understand it, the Tang Dynasty is most powerful. Since you are a trusted emissary with orders from the emperor, you must be carrying many rare treasures.

Since I'm a Buddhist, I do not cling to worldly desires or treasure.
Ha ha! I admire your modesty...
But I only ask so that we may feast our eyes.
Master! Show them your robe. They will go crazy for it.
Ha ha ha!
Wu Kong!
I don't need to see a monk's robe. I have more than 100 precious robes already.

Guangzhi! Bring some of my robes to show our guests.
Yes, Sir!

You should take a look at them.

These are the robes I have collected.
Eh?
A monk's robe need only cover the body. Why do they make such a fuss about cloth?
There are more than 200 pieces, made by the world's best tailors, using the world's best fabric.
Hey, Chief Priest!
All of these robes combined cannot match a stitch of the master's robe!
Mind your tongue!
It's true!
Liar!

It's the truth! Do you want to see it?
Fine!
So easy to trick a temperamental monkey.

Wu Kong!
What?
What makes you think you can show the robe to them without my permission?

Don't you understand that things make people greedy?
Sure ...
So reject your greed, and let me show them!

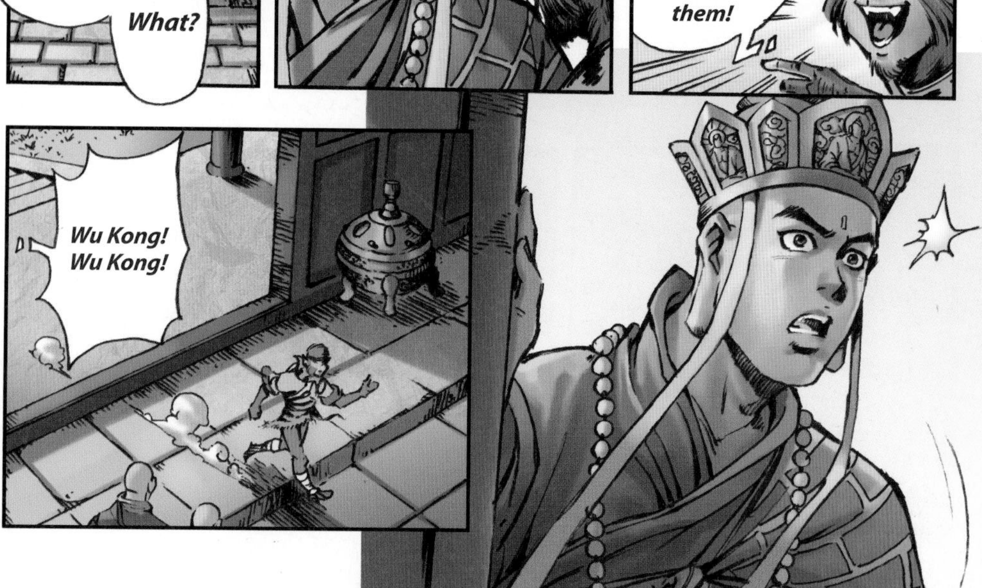
Wu Kong! Wu Kong!

Ha ha! Feast your eyes on this!
What a trouble-maker!

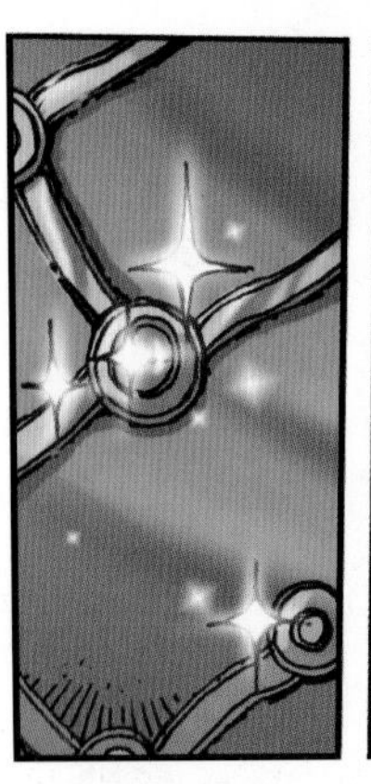

It's... beautiful. So...

...A real treasure.

In my entire life, I've never…
Please continue.
...I've never seen such a precious treasure.
I would like to be able to look at it more thoroughly.
May I borrow it and return it in the morning?
That is, um, well…
Sure you can! But it's easy to be mesmerized ...
So don't forget to return it first thing in the morning.
Sure, sure.
Priests from the Tang Dynasty truly are generous.
!
Wu Kong is making things difficult again.
Surely, it is a heavenly treasure!
It does not belong to this world.

I agree.
It seems to be an unusual thing.

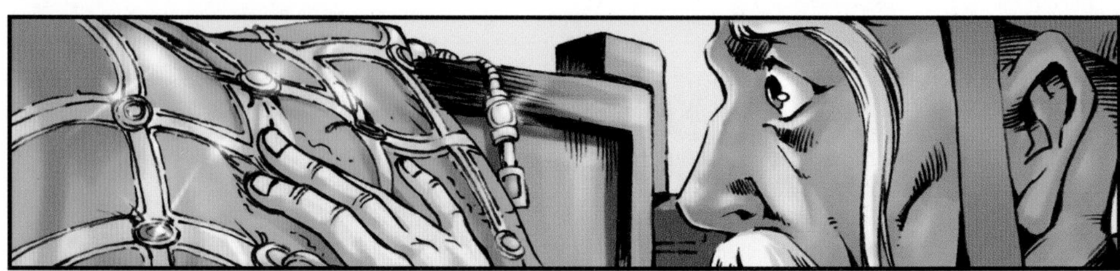

sob, sob
Chief Priest!

Why do you weep while you look at this?

I cry
because I have to give it back in the morning.
But Chief Priest...

...if it stayed a few days longer...

...you would be able to see it as much as you like.

But if it stayed for a year, I would be able to see it for a year...
...But once it leaves, I would be that much sadder.

...

I see... What about this?

You've already got the treasure...
?
So maybe we kill the visitors!

Then, the treasure will be yours forever!

Really? Can you do that?

I have a better idea.
What is it? Tell me!
Don't worry about the priest. It's the monkey we should be concerned about.
Yes. If you fail…
THERE IS A GOOD WAY TO AVOID FAILURE!
What is it? Tell me right now!

MONKEY KING

Appendix

JOURNEY TO THE WEST

At the palace of heaven, a celebration is underway. Gods, wizards, kings, and fairies bearing peaches have all gathered to revere and celebrate Buddha, who has recently purged heaven of a great menace.

Meanwhile, far below, the menace is buried beneath a mountain that Buddha created with five fingers. Sun Wu Kong, the Handsome Monkey King, who declared himself the Emperor of Heaven and repeatedly upset the heavenly order, has been punished for losing a wager made with the Buddha when the god intervened on behalf of the Jade Emperor during Sun Wu Kong's last campaign against the heavens, an attempt to overthrow the Jade Emperor himself. Sun Wu Kong almost succeeds in escaping from under the mountain by lifting it off the ground, but the Buddha places a charm, which contains the weight of the universe, on the mountain's peak.

Sun Wu Kong buckles under the weight and is pinned under the mountain in such a way that only his head is exposed.

Five hundred years later, a priest named San Zang, who is journeying to the West, comes upon Five-Finger Mountain. San Zang is a trusted emissary of the Tang Dynasty who has been sent west on the orders of Emperor TaiZong to search for the Mahayana Sutras, a Buddhist scripture revealed to the priest by the Buddhist Goddess of Mercy. The priest is led by a pack of monkeys to the base of Five-Finger Mountain and Sun Wu Kong's exposed head. The monkey explains to the startled priest that the Goddess of Mercy has already visited him, and ordered him to accompany San Zang on his journey. San Zang removes the weighted charm, Sun Wu Kong frees himself from under the mountain, and the two set out on their journey.

It is not long, though, before San Zang grows wary and then frustrated with his new traveling companion. Sun Wu Kong demonstrates impatience, a need to impress his new master by bragging about his past indiscretions, and a tendency toward violence that repulses the priest. San Zang tries to explain the importance of the scriptures they seek, and Sun Wu Kong chides him for being brought up in a Buddhist monastery. San Zang reprimands Sun Wu Kong for not having the discipline required to attain enlightenment, and then vehemently scolds him for killing a tiger and then six bandits who threatened their passage to the West. Angered by San

Zang's disciplinary lectures, Sun Wu Kong abandons his new master. San Zang continues on alone, and before long he is met by an old woman who questions him about his missing student and offers him a gift that will help to control Sun Wu Kong.

Meanwhile, the monkey has taken refuge in the palace of the Sea King, who had been terrorized by the monkey five centuries earlier. While accepting Sun Wu Kong as his guest, the Sea King very delicately admonishes him for abandoning San Zang. Using a drawing that illustrates the story of Zhang Liang as an example, the Sea King points out the virtues of serving a master, and tells Sun Wu Kong that by agreeing to the Goddess of Mercy's orders to convert to Buddhism and accompany San Zang, he is obligated to return to his master and make a genuine effort to become enlightened.

Sun Wu Kong decides to return to San Zang, and along the way he is met by the Buddhist Goddess of Mercy. Unbeknownst to Sun Wu Kong, the goddess is returning from a visit to San Zang, where she disguised herself as an old woman and gave the priest a headband that will contain Sun Wu Kong's worst impulses. San Zang tricks the monkey into wearing the headband, which the monkey struggles to take off. San Zang then utters an incantation taught to him by the Goddess of Mercy that gives Sun Wu Kong a splitting headache, and threatens to utter it any time the monkey

misbehaves.

Newly subdued, Sun Wu Kong asks about San Zang's past. The priest tells the story of his parents' tragedy and his orphaned upbringing at a Buddhist monastery, but trails off without fully explaining why things turned out the way they did.

The two come to a treacherous mountain pass. While crossing a mountain lake they are set upon by a water dragon that eats their horse before Sun Wu Kong narrowly saves his master and flies them to safety. Sun Wu Kong then returns to the lake to look for the horse, but the dragon attacks and then retreats before the monkey can defeat him. He returns to San Zang, and is about to be scolded again when the Goddess of Mercy appears to inform the duo that the dragon is called YuLong, a sea prince who was sentenced to death for causing trouble in heaven but spared by the Goddess, much like Sun Wu Kong. The Goddess tells them that their journey will require more than an ordinary horse, and she transforms YuLong into a horse to accompany them.

San Zang, Sun Wu Kong, and the dragon horse continue west, and after three days they come upon a Buddhist monastery. The chief priest of the monastery recognizes that San Zang is an emissary of the Tang Dynasty, and immediately asks the priest if he is carrying any precious treasures. San Zang answers modestly, but Sun Wu Kong almost immediately begins bragging about the monk's robe they are carrying, a garment given to San Zang by the Goddess of Mercy herself. The chief priest laughs and tells them that he has many such garments, but upon seeing San Zang's robe he becomes immediately transfixed and covetous. A couple of monks suggest to the chief priest different ways that the precious robe could be his forever; one of these plans involves killing the priest and the monkey.

THE HUMAN DRAMA OF GODS AND MONKEYS

The Journey to the West is much more than a tale about a group of people headed west in search of a precious item. It is also the story of a spiritual journey away from human traits such as ambition and pride and toward selfless enlightenment. This spiritual journey, most expressly taken by Sun Wu Kong, is one found in various mythologies when a character seeks to understand the world outside of his own desires. What makes Sun Wu Kong's spiritual journey interesting is that he is not expressly human. Born from a stone on Spring Mountain and taught the secrets of everlasting life by Master Puti, Sun Wu Kong has always occupied a place somewhere between the earth and heaven. As a result, he is the product of two competing influences, the animal desire for satisfaction and the pursuit of eternal life and wisdom. This is why Sun Wu Kong shares with humans certain characteristics, like envy and greed. Ultimately, though, what will liberate Sun Wu Kong is coming to know certain characteristics that are uniquely human, such as honor, compassion, and fidelity. If he is to complete his spiritual journey, he must come to terms with the discipline of Confucianism, Buddhism, and Taoism, the last of which is represented by Sun Wu Kong's principal adversary, the Jade Emperor.

The spiritual journey is central to The Journey to the West because, as in numerous mythologies, the heavens play an enormous role in how events unfold. Even though the gods and goddesses possess incredible power and wisdom, it falls to "human beings" to shoulder the burden of achieving their desires and the harmony they seek. In this way, the gods of The Journey to the West resemble Olympian gods, who use people like chess pieces, ever maneuvering and manipulating the fates of those selected to carry out the task. The Buddhist Goddess of Mercy does not travel to the West to retrieve the Buddhist scriptures herself; instead, she enlists a noble priest and gives him four companions she had previously recruited for the journey. Each companion is selected for a specific reason; for Sun Wu Kong, the journey is his chance to repent for the trouble he caused during his reign as the Handsome Monkey King and the Emperor of Heaven. In order to help San Zang complete the physical journey, Sun Wu Kong must not only defeat bandits and dragons who threaten their safety, he must also defeat his own selfishness, because the adversaries they encounter will not always attack

with weapons or teeth; sometimes, they will attack with covetousness, and manipulate Wu Kong's pride to attempt to rob or kill the traveling priest.

It is here that The Journey to the West is different from the Olympian myths: rather than using people as pawns in ongoing feuds between themselves, the Buddhist Goddess of Mercy and her cohort have enlisted these travelers to help them save humanity. And in order to save humanity through enlightenment, the very flawed and very human companions must first find enlightenment for themselves. Thus Journey to the West is littered with demonstrations of human virtue, such as Emperor TaiZong's commitment to the more people-oriented Mahayana Buddhism that prospered during the Tang Dynasty, San Zang's selfless offer to find the scriptures, and the story of Zhang Liang's commitment to serving his master. These people aren't perfect, nor are San Zang's almost-human companions. But they share a journey not just to the West, but toward a more fully realized humanity. The emphasis on the pursuit of goodness and selflessness is ultimately what makes The Journey to the West one of the most humane novels ever written.

SUN WU KONG

Adventures from China MONKEY KING

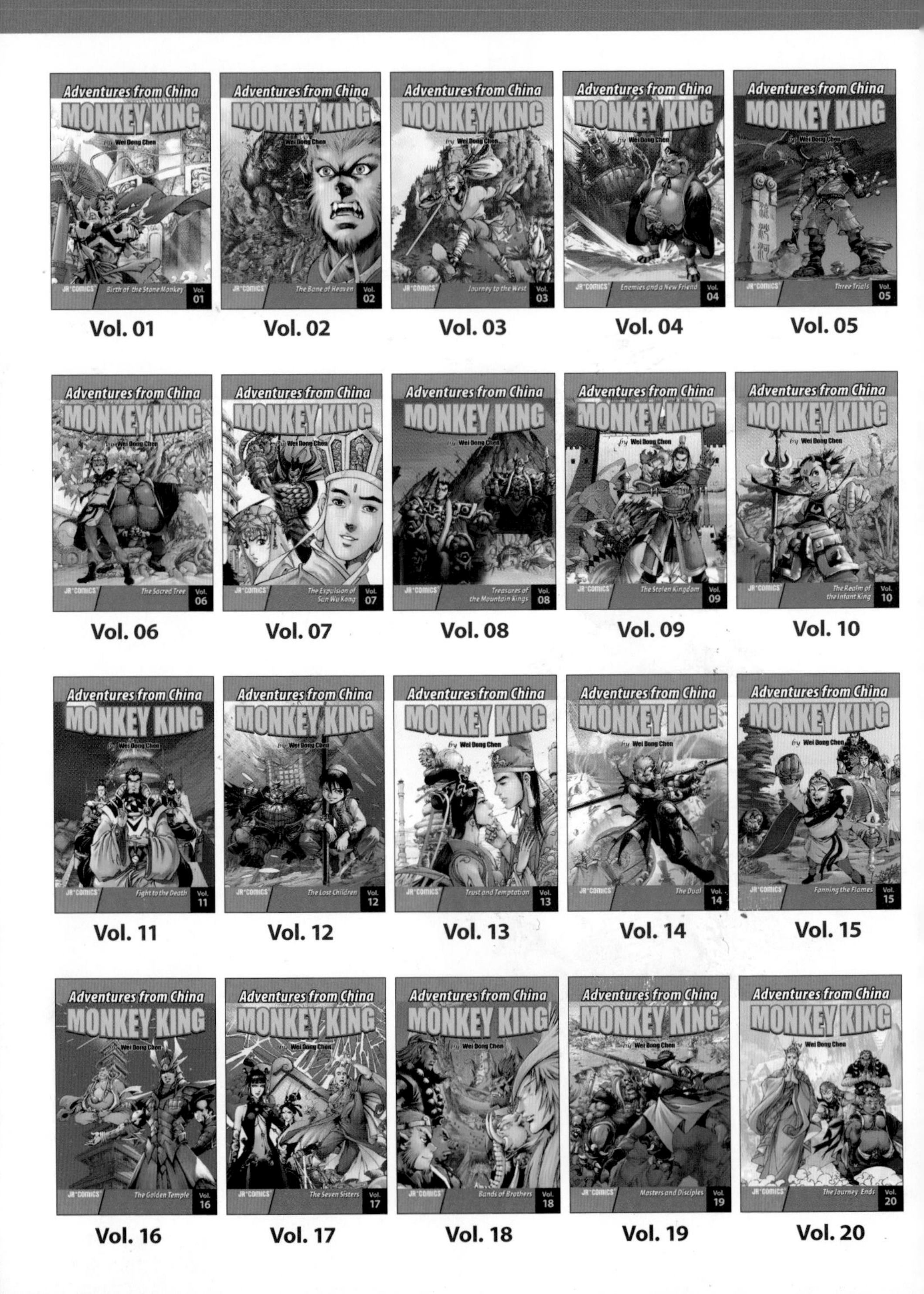